I0726944

BEFORE

the

GLORY

PRESLEY PINDER

WORKBOOK PRESS LLC
187 E Warm Springs Rd,
Suite B285, Las Vegas, NV 89119, USA

Website:	https://workbookpress.com/
Hotline:	1-888-818-4856
Email: admin@workbookpress.com

Ordering Information:
Quantity sales. Special discounts are available on quantity purchases by corporations, associations, and others.
For details, contact the publisher at the address above.

ISBN-13:	978-1-953839-43-5 (Paperback Version)
		978-1-953839-44-2 (Digital Version)

REV. DATE: 10/13/2022

DEDICATION

I dedicate this book to my deceased uncle, Osbourne Alexander Pinder who inspired me many years ago to write this book; to my wonderful parents, Stanley and Sybil Pinder; to my beautiful and faithful wife, Verla Oramae; to my six wonderful children, Phyllincia, Alvin, Brendi, Brandon, Analecia and Taquan; my second mother and prayer partner, Warrior, Cousin Rowena Cooper; and the entire Millars community family. The Good Book admonishes us in Proverbs to "Train up a child in the way he should go and when he is old, he will not depart from it".

INTRODUCTION

Some eight years ago during construction on a neighboring church in Long Island, my uncle Osbourne was helping to put the mix together for the walls. As I stood on the scaffold, my uncle looked up at me and said; "You know what? I think you should write a book. You have been through a lot in life and you have been lots of places. I think you should seriously consider writing the book."

Several years passed and the idea completely slipped my memory until December of 2018. It came with intense pressure. I began to slowly cut myself off from the world around me to draw closer to God and His Word. This intense pressure continued right up until the month of April 2019. One day while I was mowing my lawn, I prayed to God asking Him for His direction in the writing of this memoir. That is when I heard His voice in my spirit giving me the name of the book. He said, "Beyond the Glory". I knew that it had to be the plan of God. I immediately began to pray earnestly for God to direct my path. I knew God had heard my request because He had promised to give us 'the desire of our hearts'. My brother-in-law, Josh, introduced me to a family long-time friend, Mr. Neely who without hesitation promised to help me with this book as best as he could. At the time of our introduction, he had already written thirteen books, one of which is a very common book. He remembered the 1942 Hurricane and authored his best seller titled; "The Greatest and Deadliest Hurricanes of the Caribbean and the Americas. now I can say that 'Nothing is Impossible with God'. So, here I am, to God be the Glory, great things He has done. I hope and pray that this book will inspire you to inspire others. I need you to experience God and come to know that He is real and that He has a plan and a purpose for your life. So I say 'Free at last, free at last, thank God Almighty I am free at last. My prayer is that God will anoint your mind, and that the Holy Spirit will be your teacher, that the Holy Spirit will reveal truths beyond what is written here and I pray that the Lord will use this book as a tool in His hand to make you hunger and thirst for more of His absolute truth. I pray that your experience is the same with our loving Saviour.

Presley Pinder

CONTENTS

CHAPTER 1

GROWING UP IN LONG ISLAND

Home is where I went to school, where I learnt to differentiate between right and wrong, good and evil.

If this book was the Advertising Agency on the billboard for a newly found drug on the market, the doctors would have been running to explore the cure, but to God be the glory, great things he hath done.

I was born on the beautiful island of Long Island, in the year 1963 in the month of June, in the settlement of Simms. My parents are Sybil and Stanley Pinder of Millars, Ling Island. I am the third child of ten children, 6 boys and 4 girls, two of the boys are now deceased.

I received my education at Millars All Age School, where I graduated at the age of 16 years, with 7 BJCs under my belt. Some of my fondest memories are of those school days. Lots of my school friends contributed to making life fun. Two of my closest friends are dead now, but I have been left with many childhood memories still lingering in my heart up to this very day.

Growing up in Long Island was an experience that I love revisiting. When I look back at my childhood days, I see so many cherished memories with so much value that it is priceless when compared to the times that we are living in now.

Growing up in Millars was an opportunity that I look at now as a blessed community. Every single household had a Christian family. Many of the men were either pastors or somehow otherwise connected to the church. Sunday mornings would find every single child of the settlement in church, they would be there three times that day, morning, noon and night. At these services, we as children, were taught the values of life and fed the spiritual food which was the Word of God.

Back when I was growing up there was no 'Crime Watch' in our Community, because the word of God was common in every home. There was no need for outside eyes, we lived by the Golden Rule. It was natural to hear on a daily basis the memory verse from Proverbs, "Train up a child in the way he should go and when he is old he will not depart from it."

Other than having Godly parents who were the best of the best since sliced bread, I was also blessed to have spent many years with two of the best Christian Grandparents, who will always be in my heart forever. (Mrs. Rosalie & Blanch Miller, both deceased; Rev. Elisha Miller former pastor of the Salem Baptist Church and one of the past presidents of the Long Island District of Baptist Churches.

We all as children, living in Millars Long Island, had learnt the value of hard work at an early age. My dad had a trucking company that was the source of income for his family. He had no problems providing for his family…the cupboards in the kitchen were always filled and the house was always full of visitors and friends, even to this very day it still remains that way. As men and women now, we, the children still refer to the homestead as 'Little General' because it was always stocked right out. My dad was the best at whatever he attempted. He was the personification of the Lord's causing the hand to prosper. He was the perfect husband, father, and a very humble Christian gentleman. His children had no problem calling him dad. He is a man among many, because he can brag that he brought up all of his children with a steady hand. Thank you dad for a job well done.

My mom has very little to say. She was nicknamed 'Fluffy', the faithful breeder of 10 children. She is the true servant of Jesus Christ. She served the home and children with a steady hand. She is the virtuous and committed woman that any man today wishes to model his wife after. If I had to write a book on my mom and dad alone there would not be enough pages in the world to put that book together, and not enough ink either. They sacrificed much for God and their family.

Even though growing up was hard for us, we still had time to sneak out or go out to catch a game of marbles or fly kites. These were the games of the day. Many times these games caused my parents to use the rod of correction, because the national anthem in our home was "Spare the rod, spoil the child." When you look back after 56 years that national anthem proved to be the most fruitful thing ever spoken. In today's generation we see that our nation and our world is spoiled, the rod was spared too often. Sparing the rod, our schools are in trouble, our workplaces are in trouble, our teachers are in trouble. We have lost our nation and we are reaping what we have sown. We've forgotten God's law, 'to train up a child in the way he should go and when is old he will not depart from it. Today we call it child abuse. It is so sad…teenagers are committing the crimes. As a teen I could not be found outside of the home after dark, unless it was a church night and we were either going to or returning from church. So now I can say 'Thank God' to the parents of yesterday. Hats off to them, they did an excellent job. When I look back over my childhood days, I began to pick out all the valuables that I received from my parents. It has now became a treasure box that I hold dearly to myself.

My childhood days taught me how to respect myself and those who surrounded me, especially the older persons. I remember when we went to church we couldn't sleep in church. We could not chew gum, nor walk, or talk in the sanctuary. Everyone was 'ma'am or sir'. We had a gentleman called the sexton in our church, who carried a tamarind switch that was his best friend and he never failed to use it and no one called the police or cried 'child abuse'. No one played loud music while passing the church…there was respect for the house of the Lord. When men walked by, they would remove their hats to show respect. Nowadays, respect is rarely seen. No one seems to respect the house of the Lord. Children are acting and behaving in any way they choose, whether their parents are there or not. Once we were called a Christian Nation…back when people knew where their children were at all times. Now we are only carrying the name, and our ways are far it. From the very top to the bottom we have forgotten God's law to 'train up a child in the way he should go etc…Spare the Rod, spoil the child.' Now that we have spared the rod and we have spoiled the child, not only the child, but the entire nation is now in trouble. We are now reaping what we have sown, and no one wants to accept the blame. Everybody is playing the blame game. Now crime is on the rampage and our young men are dying in the streets. For now we are reaping what we have sown. God himself sum it up in His word, when he says that 'The nation that forgets God shall surely perish, all because we have disobeyed.'

CHAPTER 2

LEAVING HOME

March 2, 1982 was a joyful day and sad day for me. It was time for me to say goodbye to my island and hometown. Time had come to say goodbye to my brothers and sisters. My brother who has the oldest child, Sidney, now deceased, had already left high school for a new life in Nassau. My sister, Karen Gay, was completing her high school education in Nassaue, at the A.F. Adderlay High School. I was on my way to Matthew Town, Inagua to begin a new job and new life with a brand new family. My new family was the Pyfroms. There were mostly girls in this family, but they welcomed me into their home. At the age of 17, I had to leave my hometown, my family, and my friends. This was a very sad day.

I was accompanied on this trip by Mr. Charles Adderlay of Glintons, deceased, who was the current administrator, my mother's close relative and my former teacher. As the plane lifted off the runway at the Stella Maris Airport, it headed east. I looked at every rock until the southern tip of the island was out of sight. I wandered what was ahead. Inagua was an island that I had never visited before. I had no idea how the people looked or how they would respond to me, someone new, from another island. The question weighing my mind was 'Am I going to be ok on this strange piece of rock called Inagua?' The farther away the plant got from Long Island the more fear took a hold of me. I found a way to calm myself. If the new move does not work out, there was only 365 miles of ocean between us, I could always return home…this thought calmed me and caused me to relax because the flight still had a long way to go, we were half way there.

We landed in Inagua, it looked like Long Island…It was just big instead of long. There was only one settlement. They were mostly situated all along the western coastline. At the very northern tip there was Seymour's and at the very southern tip there was Gordons. Many other settlements settled between those two. Inagua seemed more beautiful. Upon landing we left the airport and drove straight to the administrator's residence which was situated at the very top of the only hill on the island. The house was huge, it was yellow. This was the place where my family was situated. This was home. While sitting on the porch outside, all alone, as a resident of the commissioner's home I focused my eyes on the west, in the direction of Long Island, where I knew my home was. I began to feel homesick for my parents, my brothers and sisters, my cousins, my friends and the list goes on. As the tears began to roll down my cheeks I realized that I was going to have to return home. That thought ended right then and there. The Administrator, my cousin, Mr. Adderley, called out to me to come and meet all of my cousins who all lived at the very bottom of the hill. I was wondering if they would like me and at the same time I was hoping that they would. I was excited. I walked up to the front door where I met the family and was immediately introduced. We all had mixed feelings about this new relationship. My new uncle and aunt, Arnold and Geraldine Pyfrom, both now deceased, and their beautiful daughters made me realize that Long Island and Inagua had some serious competition when it came to beautiful people. I just stared at them. Then it clicked in the back of my mind that the trip was not a bad idea after all. I began to imagine meeting all the beautiful girls and being hooked up in new relationships. After all I was almost 17 years of age and in my full prime.

The children stood staring at me; some smiled, others walked up to me and shook my hand. It broke my fear instantly. The were very nice to me and made me realize that I could live there even though it wasn't home. The girls were Valerie, she worked at BTC; then Alice, Marsha, Helen, Jenny and Debbie and Doris, the twins, little Ann and Stormy (deceased); Who was little at the time and one grandson Shadwick.

Later that day I met Adrian, one of the sons. He was thick, muscular, handsome, kind-hearted and very quiet. He only spoke when spoken to. He was hardworking and one of the nicest persons on God's green earth. Right then I saw that I had all the earthly protection that I needed in this house and outside. I met the oldest son much later he was living in Grand Bahama at that time.

That night when I lay down to sleep, all of my questions were answered. I was home away from home…for the first time since I left home that I realized that fear was gone. Inagua was the most southern island in the archipelago of the Bahamas and one of the larger ones. At that time it hosted the second largest salt factory in the world. Ninety percent of the workforce on Inagua worked for Morton Salt. The best kept secret was the wild life. There lived the prettiest birds I had ever seen, the spoon bill, the flamingo, the white crown pigeons and many more. There were wild hogs and wild donkeys. The wild hog is Inagua's favorite dish and the skin, which they call the ryne was another of Inagua's secrets, it was cooked in with the meat and soon became one of my favorite dishes.

Inagua was quiet. The people were close knit. They heard no evil. They saw no evil. No one interfered in other person's business. They had a nickname for the flamingo 'hush hush' because they were illegal to catch, and they caught them. Soon I began to match the people with the nickname 'hush hush' because they were not the gossiping type and they were not free when it came to information. What happened in Inagua stayed in Inagua. It was different from where I came from.

Shortly after moving to Inagua I got involved in construction, helping my uncle finish a house that he had started a while back. Soon after that my uncle got me a job at Morton Salt driving trucks. At the company I worked in the Diesel department for the first two weeks. There I learned about the huge trucks that I was preparing to drive. It did not take me long to fit in, because living there were people already established from Long Island. It was a great experience for me and I was eager to learn and also eager to get behind the wheel of those big trucks. Life here was different. I worked at Morton Salt, which at that time, had an employment of 500 people. There was a tuck shop where everyone bought snacks, drinks or lunch. It was situated outside the gate, but lunch bus will go into town and and go around to every house on every street and pick up the working crew's lunch from their family. The names of workers were on their bag. The bus would leave town at 11:00 a.m. with every person's lunch still hot. Wow, this was certainly different from everywhere else. At 11:00 back in town, all the women's eyes who did not work were glued to the TV screen. Back then they watched the popular series, "All My Children" and "Days Of Our Lives". No sound would be heard while they were watching these programmes. This was the favorite time for the women of Inagua. No one was allowed to interrupt until after 3:00, when it was time to begin cooking dinner for the families. The shows for that day were over an all could return to normal. Wow, back then it didn't take much to keep a whole town together. After all, like I said, it was a close knit town and everyone knew where each person was at all times. Matthew Town, the land of the 'hush mouths'.

The day came for me to get my chance to step into one of the trucks. My trainer's name was Mr. Basil Musgrove, a descendant of Exuma, my boss was Mr. Ingraham (deceased), assisting him was Mr. Joseph Lewis, a descendant of Providenciales, in the Turks and Caicos. The training was scheduled for two weeks, so they said. I got into the truck and we introduced ourselves to each other and headed out on the highway, towards the loaded salt pond. The truck had six forward gears in low gear, and six forward gears in high gear with a splitter button that would split you from to high and you shifted without the clutch. The clutch was only used for taking off and stopping. No other time, only mostly, when you were loading ships and had to climb the hopper. The first day went well. I sat in the passenger's seat and observed all that was going on, and learnt what every switch and button was for. The next morning we started out early, 5:00 a.m. I was in the truck on the way. Mr. Musgrove was driving. Suddenly he pulled on the side and invited me into the driver's seat. We drove to the pond and under the harvester, that loads the truck with salt. Mr. Edward Harris drove the harvester. He was a very serious and hardworking young man. He looked like a weight lifter who could slap two men down with one stroke. He soon became someone I could call my friend. He was honest, hardworking and a man of few words.

Like I said Inagua people speak with their hands and eyes, not so much with their mouths. That is why in the Bible it says that the wise men came from the east and not the west. We got loaded with the salt and was then on our way to the hopper. After dumping the salt into the hopper we drove to the service stationed to refuel. After fueling up, I was on my way, shifting and grinding gears along the way, but eventually I got the hang of it. The rpm guage and the shift stick went together as Mr. Musgrove taught me. When the rpm drops to a certain level then truck will shift. Listen to the sound of the engine, he said, and it will tell you when it is time to shift the truck. I spend the rest of the day listening to the engine, like Mr. Musgrove said, and by the end of the day, I was driving smoothly. My dad had a trucking company and I had worked around those trucks from the age of 7 through 16, so driving trucks was something I was used to, except that these were bigger trucks and everything worked differently. The next day, I started in the driver's seat. I was getting used to this piece of equipment, so blocked out all my fears of the trucks and its size and only the voice of Mr. Musgrove filled with instructions pounded into my skull. Soon I became an expert at driving and operating the trucks. On day three around 10:30 a.m. Mr. Musgrove said to me, "Mr. Pinder, you look like you are catching on fast." My response, "I feel comfortable that I can handle this task that is set before me". So he said, "Drop me off at the short cut, I will hang out in the mechanic's shop while you drive by yourself for a while." So I drove off all alone to face my new career and to get more acquainted with my best friend, the truck that became a part of my world.

CHAPTER 3

LIFE ON INAGUA

Inagua was nice, it was a dream come true! One week I would work from12 midnight to 1:00 p.m. The next week I would work from 4:30 a.m. until 1:00 p.m. When ships came in for salt we would drive for 24 hours. We work double shift until the ship was loaded, which ran approximately two to three days. I had the opportunity to see some of the largest cargo ships in the world, 800 feet in length. My plate was filled with my new job. Soon I was losing my fear of Inaguans and for my job, and also losing the longing for returning home. Inagua was great! I worked on weekdays and went to church on Sundays. Zion Baptist is now my home away from home church. The pastor at that time was the Reverend Godfrey Bain, a decent and upright man of God, with a beautiful family who at time all served and worshipped God.

Saturdays was family hunting time. The males all would go to the south eastern point of the island. We would go striking for the box fish one weekend, and the next weekend we would be hunting the wild hogs. My uncle was a hunter. He taught all the males in the family how to hunt, kids and grandkids alike. Everyone had their own gun. My favorite was the old Tom, a 12 gauge shotgun. It had the longest barrel I had ever seen. I had a very long range and carried a magazine with three 12 gauge shells. This was our sniper weapon. It had a range longer that the regular 12 Gauge five shooter pump action and it had my name on it. I loved that gun. That gun loved me. It was my world. So you see, my life was full of activities and I soon forgot about Long Island. Only now and again my mind would wander on my family back home.

Living on Inagua now was worth waiting for. New job, new family, new friends. It was fun. Work during the week, hunts on Saturdays and church on Sundays. One of the things that I experiences was that when Sunday mornings came around I did not have any pressure from anyone about going to church, because when Sunday mornings use to come around I could still hear my dad's voice saying "It's time to go to church". Then I began to understand what it meant to say, "Train up a child in the way he should go, and when he is old and he will not depart from it." Church was a must. Now, I am 165 miles away, and it is still in my head. The Bible does not lie, so I had to obey the voice in my head and head on over to Zion Baptist every Sunday morning. Most of the locals took time out to worship God on Sundays. They separated their time for God, which I respected. From the oldest to the youngest, from the top to the bottom. Did I say they were perfect in all their ways? No! They partied on week ends, they sang and they danced. They had fun. They had a standard of moral living. They did everything in order, and that's what made them different from most other islands. So here I am repeating myself with "Wise men do come from the east."

I remember one Sunday, I was invited to the Anglican Church, St. Andrews, on top of the hill and the next to the school by a friend. It was the first time I had every taken part of their worship. In the middle of the service, they had the greetings of the peace. Everyone moved, they came around the entire congregation and hugged each other. In my church back home that was done at the end of the service so when it happened in St. Andrews that morning, I left through the back door when I was finished hugging everyone. I headed home, which was at the bottom of the hill. My friend saw me, ran me down and said that the service was not over, that was just the greeting of the peace. Wow, shame on me. I headed back, went up the steps and back into the church. That was my first mistake while living on Inagua.

This new life was overwhelming, I was in Paradise, at least I thought so at that time. For the first time, I was working, making my own money. Life was at its best. We had a flying bank, RBC, that came in every Friday morning and left that afternoon. Which opened a new door of opportunities for me. I was not only able to open a bank account, but I could send money back to my parents to help with the remaining siblings. I was really feeling great about myself and the responsibilities I had taken on. I had great memories on both islands and great friends. Who could ask for more? As time went on I returned home to visit whenever I got free time from work. My mom would always say "I am so proud of you", my little sisters, Stephanie, Bloneva, and Florence would say, "You are the best brother in the whole wide world." Their writings were hard to understand, they were still in primary school. They were filled with love. I would isolate myself whenever I received parcels from home, because I knew I would be crying, because of all the love inside. I missed them so much, but I knew it was time to grow up and be the man my dad had thought me to be. It was also then, that I had found out from my mother that I had a daughter born back home. My new life now had taken away a lot of the empty void in my life. It was now a place of great and memorable memories. To this day my love of home and family is just as strong. I had to accept the plate as it was served. Inagua was my home. Different people, a different family, a new way of life, all on one plate and all at the same time. Moving forward not realizing that this was about to all turn around in so many different form and fashion before the day was over. Inagua was a great life! Soon my homesick days were gone and I was now enjoying my new home, new family, new job, new friends. For the first three years, it was almost perfect.

One Saturday afternoon, three years later I was invited to a party by one of my friends, a coworker's sister was having a house party just across the street from my uncle's hose on Queen's Highway. It was a typical Saturday afternoon and lots of persons attended. After a while I got tired of standing around, so I went with two of my girlfriends on a bench next to the house. My coworker came over to me and said "Looks like you're bored, so I have something to liven you up." In a plastic container there was some soft, white powdery stuff which I soon learned was cocaine, something I had never seen before or experienced. I was told to sniff it, it was supposed to wake me up and get rid of the sleep. "It's just a party drug," he said, not knowing that my life would be changed in so many different ways. I did what I was told being the curious person that I am and it did what he said it would do. I was not sleepy or tired any more. I returned to the bench with my two friends and we drank beers and chatted for a long, long time. When the night was finally over, I went home to my bed, not knowing that the spirit that I had inhaled into my body would be with me and become another best friend and change me in so many different ways.

Life went as usual. Work, church, family; helping the family in Long Island. But I noticed that my Friday night outings were increased more than usual…my life was soon changing right in front of my eyes. Life went on a normal for a while. Soon this dedicated, young, vibrant worker was living like Scarface, he couldn't wait for weekends to come and nights to go by the club. Parties were often held in Inagua. Back in the early 80's parties were the norm…you could bet every weekend, there would be one somewhere. They were dedicated to their work, but when weekend came they would enjoy themselves. Not everyone, but certainly most of the younger ones. My life at this time was hard, the relationship that I was in at the time produced a 9lb baby boy. I had to work night shift, spent long hours driving the big salt trucks on dangerous roads. There were empty roads trucks going into the pond, and loaded roads coming out of the pond, and a twenty-foot ditch between the roads. So if you drop sleep for a second, you were dead. I loved driving those big trucks, even now. I don't drive those trucks anymore but I was a great driver.

One particular memory that stands out more than any other is: my truck suddenly stopped on an empty road heading to the pond to be loaded, several miles away from the mechanic's shop, almost at the very end of the pond heading to town. It would only move in the reverse gear, no forward gear, an obvious transmission problem. The main road was far away from me. This incident happened around 10 a.m. Shortly after I asked a coworker take a message to the mechanic's shop for someone to come and check. Our shift would be finished at 1:00 p.m. I waited and waited. Nobody came. Soon 11:30 a.m. came and I knew that I had to make a decision. I did something that took lots of guts, no driver had every attempted to do what I was going to do. I believe that I set a record that day that would never be broken. I put the truck in reverse and drove backward, knowing that if I had made one mistake I couldn't fix it plus the 20 foot ditch was yawning for me. I started out very slowly. All the other drivers, my coworkers, could see what I was attempting to do, some slowed down as they passed, others honked their horns. Soon I was at the main road, and on my way down the highway towards the mechanic's shop. I was finally off the death threat road…there were now spectator's watching. The mechanic's met me three quarter's of the way…instead of stopping me to check the truck, they drove behind me. Everyone wanted to see if this was possible. By then I had reached a sharp corner to the shop and I took it slowly. I straightened the vehicle and went through the gate and into the mechanic shop's door. My boss at that time was Mr. Joseph Louis, my son's grandfather, deceased, and someone who I had become proud to know, asked me how I had gotten there, I told him that I had to reverse the truck here and he said that he didn't believe it, so I showed him the truck. He told me that that was great. Drivers at Morton Salt never believe for one day that you are not respected, because I have been down the roads that you drive now. I have driven up the hoppers to load ships. I have taken tractors all alone up to the top of the high salt heaps to push the salt for the excavators to load the trucks. I have driven your harvesters at night. I have done it all, so hats off to you. You are the best since sliced bread. Now I am a Christian and my will and desire is to pray for you every day and night, that God will keep you and your family and all those who handle heavy equipment and work at the great Morton Salt Company from the top to the bottom.

The party grew to a point where I soon started missing days and nights at work. I was soon called in to the office and was told that I had to get it together. Soon after many attempts to change my life my great job and career was over. One morning when I awoke I heard these words in my head, "I will arise and go to my father, and say father I have sinned against heaven and against earth and I am no longer worthy to be called your son." I was soon on my way back home. Inagua now was about to become a memory. The life, the people, the job. My son who was now continuing to grow up was about to start school without me…All the dreams and the ambition was gone. I could not take care of myself nor could I take of my son. My life was a mess and I was asked by myself and others to take time off and get it together.

CHAPTER 4

BACK HOME

Soon I was standing back on the shores of Long Island. I remember the words of the matriarch, Ruth, in the Bible when said, "I went out full, and I came back empty." I had let my family, my sibling, my community and my friends down. Most of all I had let myself down. It was over and I felt as if I had reached the end of the rope. I sat down that evening in my father's house and said; I have messed up the only opportunity I had of being somebody in life. How many of us Satan is talking to right now telling us that we have missed your only chance at life.

But I heard the Lord say "I am a God of second chances!" He does not care how far we have been or what we have been through, He said, "In fact I will give you back the years that the canker worm and wild locusts have stolen from you." He reiterates that if you confess your sins then He is faithful and just to forgive you of those sins. He wants you, His sons and daughters to give Him your hearts. That is all He wants, your hearts. Give him your heart today, I promise you he will never, ever let you down.

I was back home and like many of you right now are saying, Father I have sinned against you and I am not worthy to be called your son. It is over for me. I have let myself down. I am beyond forgiveness and I have gone too far. But little did I know, God had kept me alive just to let me know that my purpose here on this earth has not begun as yet. All of my past were stepping stones that one day I was going to look back and say with assurance that what the enemy had meant for bad, God had His plan to turn it around for His good. I understand now that God knows our ending from our beginning for our lives.

So after a month or two of just doing odd jobs around the home and the community, I was able to get a job driving a truck for a food-store and lumber yard. The year was 1989, September when I started. Soon I was okay again, driving from one end of Long Island to the next. When the weekends came the partying was still there…the women, the drugs and the cold beers became a part of my life again. It was fun for me. Club Thompson Bay was the Friday Night Spot, I rarely missed their dances. Regattas, homecoming being at all the hot spots lasted for two years and then in 1991, I was offered an operating job for one of the top divers in Salt Pond. It was a hard job, long hours and tiring work, but the paycheck was great. We worked from sun up until sun down. I realized that only hard work would bring great success.

Staying sometimes out to sea for more than two weeks at a time became tiresome. At the end of the first season in July of 1992 I was offered a job in Exuma with a local pastor of Long Island, who was building a home in Forbes Hill.

CHAPTER 5

LIVING IN EXUMA

Living on Exuma was not a bad life at all. We pretty much, just me and the pastor, built the home by ourselves. The building was up and soon it was finished. He moved back to long island and because I was offered a job in Georgetown, I stayed. I now worked on a two-story plaza 'Around the Corner' next to the Edgewater Restaurant & Bar. The partying continued, the women and the drugs. After the first year I was blessed again with a never mind leave it in daughter and another year later a second son. Now four children are here on three different islands. It was time to hang it up and move back home. I moved back to Long Island and soon moved to Glintons, with my maternal grandparents, now deceased, to work for Cape Santa Maria. The Cape had just been bought by a new owner and was beginning with new construction and renovations. I worked in Construction and as a bonefish guide.

CHAPTER 6

HOME TO STAY

My new job at the Cape Santa Maria, I was placed in training to learn how to become a bonefish guide, something I was not familiar with. This profession became a hobby and a life-long occupation. It was okay, but soon after I returned to my first love, masonry, for the new buildings. So I did both. Both were great in their own way. Soon the construction had my full attention. I was doing most of the mason work on the newly constructed buildings, after-all, it was the first trade my dad had me take up upon completion of high school in 1979.

Living in Burnt Ground I met a lady who was living directly in front of my grandparents. She was a primary school teacher at that time at the Glinton's Primary School. She is now retired after 42 years of teaching. At that time neither of us knew that we would someday marry. We talked, hung out, cooked and went to church together. Sometimes she would come and help my grandmother. She is a singer and very respectable young lady in the community. Not knowing that this was the end of the single life for me, I thought to myself that she was the person that would straighten me out. Within one year we were married and settled down…at least I thought so. Soon after, she gave birth to two children, with one year between, making me the father now of 6 beautiful children, 3 boys and 3 girls whom I love dearly.

In spite of all the different islands working and moving it was constantly spoken over my life that God had a calling for my life. He had a great work for me to do even in my wayward ways and my prodigal son life in and out of the hog pen. I keep hearing the still small voice saying, "This is not the life I have called you to do." But no matter how high or low I got in life God was always with me and always protecting me for such a time as this. He said in His word that the work that I have started in you, I will see to completion. Now looking back over my life I know now why I did not overdose, die in a car crash…never allowed the enemy to take my life. Maybe without any question I was the Bahamian Saul.

Still working and trying to live a secret life and put on a good front, hiding my inner secrets, the drugs the women and the beers never stopped me from going to church. I never, in all my days, forgot the home training. But my love for the world kept calling me. In June of 2000 I moved into my new home with my wide and two kids. The triplex situated in Millars Long Island, east of queens highway, One side was live-able, not quite finished, but it was home, our home, with a beautiful front yard where we still reside at this day. Our kids are gone, but it is still home for the two of us, my wife and I. Sometime it is home for church friends, families and even outsiders, so even in my wayward ways God has been good to me.

I was home back in the community where my parents live, and any grown man and woman out there knows, no matter how old you get parents never absent themselves from their children's lives, especially children of Christian parents. My parents are still alive, so I say this day, "Thank God, they are still alive and in good health." I started going back to my church as often as I could. It is so good to be back home. I began to realize in a small way that this was the plan of God. He allowed me to go through many things and visited many islands, but He brought me back exactly where he wanted me to be, back home in my own native ground. Even the constant church attendance did not stop the partying. Even being married with kids did not stop the partying. Everything now was in the open, my life was not a secret anymore. I kept working and painting this pretty picture of my life. I struggled through my habits and the struggle was real. I kept hearing the voice of God in the back of my head "One day I'm going to trade this old cross for a crown". Sunday school was my favorite time of the service and still is. I manage to bring my kids up in church, with God's help. I would take them to church almost every Sunday. My wife, a member of Church of God of Prophecy, went to her own church every Sunday, but the kids went with me to the Baptist. After they grew up, my son went with his mom, but my daughter, Annalicia stayed with me. She, from a child, never left my side, right up to this day. Struggling in and out of church, week after week, month after month, year after year could not get it together. Sometimes my marriage was up on the rocks, other times it was okay…but through all the bad times God kept bringing us together. This happened so many times that I began to see that love does cover a multitude of sins.

Even then I was asked to help in church; teach Sunday school, speak sometimes. My life was still a rollercoaster. Many nights I would come in after partying and I would pray and say "Lord, this is not the life that you have for me. Nor is it the one that I want." And then it happened.

December 2018 and my world is turned upside down. Everything in my life was going wrong. My business was in trouble, but I still did not surrender my life completely to God. I got through Christmas, and then January, almost convincing myself to give up and die. It was as if I had nothing else to live for. But I managed, even without noticing that God was still with me and then it happened. On the 7th of February, 2019 at 10:00 a.m. I sat in my back door and I said, "Lord if you take me out of this mess that I'm in I would serve you for the rest of my life." At that moment I surrendered my life totally to Him and instantly a sweet peace came over me. I was not afraid anymore. I felt a peace that nothing in the world could give me. No drug high felt this good, I was basking in God's love and His forgiveness. I knew instantly that God had saved me and He had heard my prayer and had forgiven me and now I am a child of God. I started doing everything that God had asked me to do. My house became a home. Then slowly, day by day, month by month I was beginning to be noticed by my friends and family. I became the spiritual pillar of strength for my family. I was slowly becoming the stone that the builder had refused and was now becoming the head cornerstone. Church and God's business was becoming my passion. I was finally living what I sang and spoke about. My love for Christ started to uplift my friends and family that Christ was for everyone and not just for me. Truly God has given me the keys for the Kingdom and now He has blessed me with a great ministry. I get to teach Bible Classes three night per week in three different churches apart from my church in the northern part of the island. God is working and awesome role in and through my life for His kingdom. Now I can say like the Apostle Paul, I'm not ashamed of the Gospel of Christ. I can stand up and say to young men and women that the wages of sin is death, but the gift of God is eternal life. So, you see, my life was a roller coaster, from one place to the next, but God's love found me one day and He did not ask where I had been or why I had done what I did. Instead he said, "Come unto me all ye that are heavy burden, and I will give you rest, take my yoke upon you and learn of me, for my yoke is easy and my burden is light." So my friends, I am not ashamed to give you my life story. To God be the Glory, great things He hath done. So you see, my friends, there is no distance, no barrier that God cannot reach. All you have to do is give is give Him your heart and all these promises in His word will be yours. God has found me even when my life was in a mess. You have taken so many chances on things in your life, and you continue to take these chances. I entreat you, my friends to take a chance on God. He says come now and let us reason together, even through your sins be as scarlet, I will make them like snow.

CHAPTER 7

RE-COMMITTING YOUR LIFE

I often go to the north side, against the ocean. As I walk along the beaches to go diving, I will always tell stop for a few moments and take the time to pick up the pieces of sea glass that are washed up on the shores by the strong waves. As I look at them, in my mind, I always stop and wonder where the sea glass originates. To the common eyes these are considered rubbish, but for a person like me, I see them as beautiful treasures. Some are as big as rocks, others as small as a grain of sand. Sea glass comes from glass bottles discarded in the ocean, that are broken into pieces by the pounding surf and clashing waves. It is then polished by the constant friction of sand and surrounding elements. The sharp, rough edges are then worn down to a smooth treasure like they are. The longer it stays in the turning sea, the more beautiful it becomes. For most people they don't pay any attention to sea glass. For the most parts they are hardly noticed. Folks attach no value to them. What they see as rubbish I look at and see an amazing treasure. The reason I find sea glass so amazing is that It reminds me of God's amazing grace. These broken sea glass remind me of how God can bring beauty out of brokenness. How he can take something that has been destroyed and discarded and polish it down and make it an attractive treasure. My friends if you are anything like me, I have made many mistakes, you have made many mistakes in your life. Perhaps you have been abused and discarded by others as worthless, and just as freshly broken glass piercing the broken feet of the innocent bystander, maybe your brokenness you have cut others by your words, action and deeds. Maybe your sharp words have cut someone close to you, like a spouse, a parent or a child or a friend or an enemy for that matter, and because of that there are wounds that was left behind. You know we have all done things in our brokenness stage that we regret. Things that we cannot go back and change. They say "hurt people hurt people". That is our human nature. Even the best of us have made mistakes. We have all done things that have triggered more pain in our world today, but here is the good news. There is a God who can bring beauty out of brokenness. Our Lord desires to polish us and to smooth out our rough edges, and even then though, we are broken, we are still his precious treasures and like the tiny specs of sea glass in the sand we are not too small for Him to not notice us. He sees our brokenness, He takes special interest in our pain. God does not cause our pain, nor does He waste them. He uses them to bless others. For He is the God who can bring beauty out of brokenness. Broken hearts, broken dreams, broken lives and broken promises, all of these can become eternal blessings. The Bible say in Psalms 34: "For God is near to them who have a broken heart and saves such with a contrite spirit. Many are affliction of the righteous but the Lord delivers him out of them all." Sometimes God redeems your story, by surrounding you with people, who needs to hear your past so that it would not become their future. From the mess of brokenness, God can bring a message of blessing and from earthly he can bring heavenly triumph. From increasing pain, HE can bring eternal peace. From a brutal test, the Lord wants to bring a beautiful testimony. I am not speaking from the top of my head. I am speaking from my own personal experience and this is what God has done for me. For one day I too was a broken and discarded vessel, before the Lord found Me. I was wasting my mind on drugs, alcohol and pretty women. I was around persons with rough edges. I was a broken glass in the pile of broken glass. For many saw me as a problem child, but God saw me as potential. Where people saw trash, God saw treasure. I was immersed in His sea of love, baptized in the ocean of His grace, and to say the least, because of Jesus Christ, my life has never been the same again. What God has done for me, surely He can do the same for you. So my friends when Jesus hung on Calvary's Cross, He was assaulted by our sins, He was crushed by our condemnation, battered by our guilt and shame. His body was bruised and His heart was broken and yet He was willing to take on our guilt and shame in order to save us. We were worth it to Him, and through His brokenness, we became blessed. Today, I invite you to give to God the broken glass of your life. Give to Him your beating heart, Your broken dreams, your broken promises and I promise you that whatever your situation is, was or will be, it is not beyond salvaging. You are more than the sum of your past mistakes. It is not too late and you have not gone too far, so I say to you today that you should let the Lord use you. Let him polish you so that you can reflect his beauty in the world of brokenness. Amen

CONTACT THE AUTHOR

You can email the author at

Presley@anniescarrental.com

Telephone number

242.809.1623

Or

242.436.7445

REPEAT THIS PRAYER

Father in the name of Jesus

I confess right now, that I am a sinner,

I repent of all my sins,

Put within me a clean heart and a sound mind,

I confess with my mouth and believe with my heart,

That you have risen from the dead, and operate in my life,

I thank you Lord that you have saved me,

In the name of Jesus Christ our Lord,

AMEN